Julia Evelyn Ditto Young

The Story of Saville

Julia Evelyn Ditto Young

The Story of Saville

ISBN/EAN: 9783744707893

Printed in Europe, USA, Canada, Australia, Japan

Cover: Foto ©Andreas Hilbeck / pixelio.de

More available books at **www.hansebooks.com**

THE STORY OF SAVILLE: Told in Numbers by Julia Ditto Young

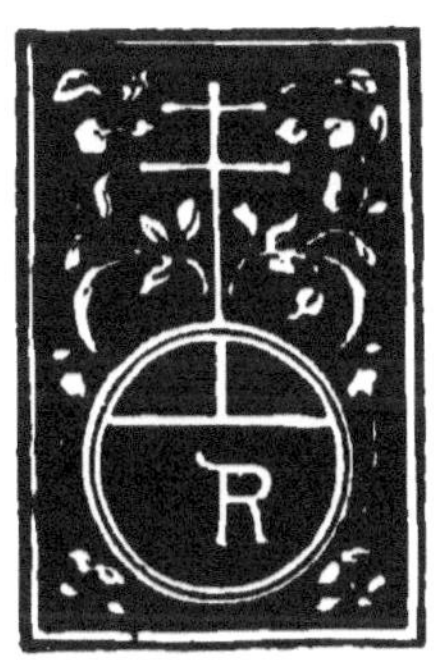

DONE INTO A BOOK AT THE ROYCROFT
PRINTING SHOP, EAST AURORA,
NEW YORK, U. S. A.
MDCCCXCVII

Of this edition but four hundred copies were printed and types then distributed. Each copy is signed and numbered and this book is number

To be blind and to be loved—what happier fate!

VICTOR HUGO.

TO THOMAS HARDY.

So dear hath grown thy rubied page to me,
When brooky wood or laughing mead I see,
Not of itself I think, but first of thee,—
And sweet is it, thus in men's eyes to hold—
Ah, moment proud!—thy strong right hand in mine,
The hand so lavish of poetic gold,
So prodigal of honey and of wine.

SAVILLE

CROUCHED like a moribund lion, wounded, alone in his lair,
Bowed 'neath unbreakable fetters, choked with an iron despair,
Wearily, heavily 'ware of the clock's dull ponderous rune
Telling how hideous morn gives birth to misshapen foul noon,
Who yet wears a loveliness regal, a beauty transcendent and bright,
Compared to her utterless offspring, the Ethiop horror of night,
Kyrle sat, scarce caring to keep account of the hours and the days,
As a rock-spitted ship need reck never more of the wind and its ways—
Sat in his isolate chamber, lost in the clamant strange town
Where he had crept in the dark when his sun forever went down,

Broken winged crept to be free of the well-meant
pity of friends
Rough as a blundering touch on a burn that
solace intends,
Free of condolences oily, felicitous, falser than
hell,
From men who at last might eclipse him, who
still rode safe on the swell,
Free of the bitter black sense—the shock—that
no one of them all
Vitally cared if he starved in his garret, a rat
in the wall.

Oh! if a merciful God, my friend, hath guer-
doned and blest you so,
Hath out of a million languid hearts, faint pulsing, feeble and slow,
Singled one scarlet treasure, that beats as strong-
ly and true
As the passionate powerful ocean-throb, for you
and only you,
That hushes its lilt to a lullaby, soothing you
while you sleep,
And bursts to blossom under your smile, and
bleeds if ever you weep,
Trample it not, nor esteem it a pebble paltry
and cheap,—

Think not twice in a life to find such a rose-
ruby to keep!

Ah! they were saying carelessly, back in his
wonted place,
"Wonder where he has slipped to? Poor devil,
he's out of the race—
Nothing remains, as the French say, but drawing
the sheet o'er the face,"—
And ever he mused of his village home and the
graves on the churchyard hill,
Where the only hearts that had beat for him
were crumbling, cruelly still,
And his useless eyes brimmed over with tears,
and slowly his blood grew chill.

Then sudden he rose and flung off his mood, and
called with a bitter laugh
For raiment against the javelin cold, for a guide
and his brand new staff,
And donning the garments doubtfully, with
timid questioning touch,
Now sharply chiding his helper, now thanking
him over much,
And groping his way before him in spite of the
lad's firm clutch,
He reached the street and onward dragged, com-
manding to be led where

The city's din was heard no more, and all the
world was fair,
For he thought that mayhap in a purer air a
Gilead-grace might be,
And God might somehow permit him to breathe
the beauty he could not see.

When he had forced his hesitant feet to traverse
a mile or so
Of street that merged in a country road, its ruts
all softened with snow,
They came to a widely sloping space and lofty
ancestral trees
That bowed in a stately welcome under a gentle
breeze,
And the lad pushed open a high arched gate and
boldly leading him through
Guided the man to a rustic bench screened by a
sturdy yew.

"Leave me here for an hour," said Kyrle, and
when he was quite alone
Sat in a hopeless silence with a face like a carven
stone,
Though once he smiled at a thought, and the
smile more pitiful was than a groan,
For scarce was it matter for mirth, how his mind
would circling rehearse

The iterant rankling venom of an inquisitorial
curse,
A special and general ban; and he deemed it
better had been for him
To have undergone impossible pangs and tor-
tures fiendish grim,
That one by one they had ravished forth each
keen particular hair,
That redhot pincers had nipped his flesh and
torn his nerve-cells bare,
That a thousand needles had stung his flesh with
delicate devilish care.
If so they had spared his eyes,—his eyes, that
were worth more then
To the wretched groveling world than the eyes
of his fellow-men,
For Oh! in this visionless later day was any so
quick as he
To snare and pinion the beauty that floats on
turret and crag and tree,
That is as the sand on the beaches, the blossoms
of foam on the sea,—
Yet he had perceived not alone this fairness outward and free,
The heritage common to all mankind, that children or clowns may prize,
But the deeper intent, the message occult, the
truth esoteric that lies

Hidden from all but a poet's soul and heaven
anointed eyes.

And now he had come to regret the fierce fanged
physical pain
That for long, long weeks had maddened, had
seethed and swirled in his brain,
Whose pressure was past enduring, whose passing was blest relief,
Yet whose worst throes seemed now more kind
than this unbearable grief,
This travail and sweat of spirit, where the uni-
verse seemed to swim
In hatefullest frantic chaos, a lunatic's furious
whim.
Strange! that because of a trifling loss, scarce
more in creation's scheme
Than a gnat in a summer woodland, a leaf afloat
on a stream,
Because two vials were shattered, God's purposes
high should seem
Only an idiot babble heard in a horrible dream.

But as he impotent girded and railed, and longed
to stifle his care
In the dull narcotic round of his room, and counted the winter air

Harsh, unbreathable, nettle-rough, suddenly was
he aware
Of a footstep light yet resolute, a beautiful woman's tread,
He knew by the keen unwonted thrill that over
his senses sped,
The silken swish, the odor sweet, and stricken
he bowed his head
Lest he be known for a sightless clod and all of
his sorrow be read.

And so she passed, but again did turn, he knew
though he could not see,
And drifted by as antelope-swift as downiest
snow-flakes be,
And laid with an instant timorous touch some
roses upon his knee,
And butterfly light and daintily still she flut-
tered upon her way,
" A rifle smoke blown through the woods for a
moment,—a moment, but never to stay!"

And he snatched the clustered loveliness up, and
sudden it seemed a part
Of his wretched life, like a dream of love in an
old man's withered heart,
A rosary dearer than beads of olive were ever to
kneeling nun,

And sweet it was to remember that faithfully soil
and sun
Had labored together in his behalf and these
fragrant globes had spun,—
And over his hand the petals curled, like a
baby's fingers weak;
And dewily kissed like a maiden's lips his sal-
low aud sunken cheek,
And all that night by his wakeful bed they
flooded the comfortless spot
With spice, and he mixed again in his mind the
crimson he had forgot,
And turning and tossing as needs he must, it all
but soothed him to know
That the utterly perfect queenly things, beautiful, all aglow,
Were close beside him, shaking out with each
waft of their rich perfume
A message of pity and tenderness across the
midnight gloom.

II.

WELL,—to a man in a dungeon an infinitesimal thing
Looms large as the fate of an empire doth to a fetterless king,
And for the first time in aeons Kyrle felt a surcease of pain,
Casting the slough of his anguish a blessed brief hour or twain,—
'Twas something to hope and to live for, that hour in the afternoon,
To question if fate would vouchsafe him a second such velvety boon,—
He would not fail to keep tryst,—not he! And yet—O heaven!—and yet—
What? had he sunk to this estate? to care if some selfish coquette,
A pampered doll, an idol of clay, born only to drive men mad,
Yielded or not to such sweet ruth as yesterday she had?

She came, with her printless hurrying feet stepping so shamed and fast
Scarce had he guessed her near him at all ere she had onward passed,
And when she had turned and again approached it seemed that she would have gone

Straight on unseeing across the stretch of wide snow-sprinkled lawn,—
But she was perforce constrained to pause; he wist not that he held up
A visage stamped with an awful need, like a beggar's holding a cup—
He never knew that he reached his hand, while slowly advanced the maid
And into his fingers eager and worn a bunch of violets laid—
And he tried to mutter a word of thanks, and he heard a quick low sob,
And he sank half stunned to his seat again, afraid of his heart's wild throb,
And it was over, all over and past! and now for twenty-four hours
He must live like a starving sailor, on a breath and a knot of flowers,
And ever there rang in his weary brain, the roar of the city above,
These words of a laurelled master, till he sickened with terror thereof,
" Hath man not evil enough, O Earth, that thou must lay on him love?"

III.

NOT amid volleying thunder, 'mid smoke-wreaths murkily dim,
Not in the fury of battle one writeth a battle hymn,
Nor chanteth of garlanded Autumn's purple and golden store,
Foison of fruit and grain and nut, till harvesting days be o'er,
And not of the glorious tempest's rage while yet the shuddering ship
Is laboring through the surges with headlong hurricane dip,
And black the skyline swings and swirls to a tremble of silver foam,
Not of the creamy blossomy death one singeth till safe at home—
Yet oft a mariner, rugged and bronzed, who joys in the tales he tells
Of plumy palm trees, brown bright maids, pink corals, and filagreed shells,
And perils of rocks, and wondrous 'scapes from famine and fever hells,
Will mark his listeners' starting eyes, happy to hold them thrall,
Yet murmurs, "Well, thank God I am here, safe sheltered among you all—

But Oh! to be back at sea, half starved, and
drenched in a sudden squall!"

Alas! for any who come to be post-graduates in
the art
Of subtle and sympathetic search in the deeps
of the human heart,
For Oh! they not so ravishing high, so thrilling-
ly, tenderly low
Could sing had they not outlived the theme
some dozen of years ago—
Alas! for them who clasp no hand, but an empty
shrivelling glove,
And remember how sweet it was last year, how
piercingly sweet to love—
And alas for the desolate souls who feel that the
rosy boy lies hid,
Quiver and dimples and wandering wings, under
a coffin lid!

But to my story. Kyrle, poor Kyrle, crept out
of his smothering mood,
The vile cocoon the worms had spun of anguish
and solitude,
And weak as an insect crawled about and struggled to find a light
Of hope or of faith or of anything sweet let into
the fathomless night.

Ah me! it had been but a struggle all through,
a moiling and rigorous life
From the early days on the niggard farm, the
petty ignoble strife
'Gainst narrow prejudice, ignorance, greed, to
wrest for himself a chance
For study and travel, for buffeting fate and con-
quering circumstance;
Then years in the studios foreign and quaint,
when salient and eager his mind
Grasped and garnered all manner of truths—ex-
cept that he had not dined;
But that's a detail, a mere trifle—the worship-
ping student will find
Diviner delight, a more rapturous joy in an intellectual stride,
A tint, or a chord, or a line in an ode, than in
aught under heaven beside;
And then the homecoming, the hopeful return to
the generous land of his birth,
The vehement passion for art, the desire to show
what he was worth,
Kaleidoscope pageants of fancies circling and
swift in his thought,
Tissues of gossamer golden freaked, with pearls
and emeralds wrought,
A bright panoramic succession, like raindrops
of April clear,

Thicker than jewels of August dew, so that his only fear
Was that the phantom embryos, tiny as stars of snow,
Might melt and slip away into naught, and he never see them go—
And often he rose in the dead of night and dashed off a virile sketch
To lull into quiet some clamoring shape that had kept his mind at a stretch;
Then followed his masterpiece, "Rupert's Trust,"—God! how he sweated and slaved,
Denying his body forgotten the nurture and slumber it craved;
Ah! that was well worthy the doing, worthy a continent's praise—
Men for a slighter achievement than this had been crowned with eternal bays—
He had dropped his palette and brushes, had sent his soul in the gaze
He bent on his picture completed, his beautiful darling,—had smiled
To think that his wedlock devoted had bloomed in an exquisite child,—
What! could it be that men cherished their children born but of the flesh
As he cherished this holier offspring snared in a mystical mesh,

The child of himself and of Love,—deep love for his race and his art,
And for whatsoever of good and pure in this our being hath part,—
And then, while he gazed exalted and rapt, perceiving the glory-rays
Stream meteor-like from the picture and merge in an opaline haze,
Sudden the haze was a thunder-cloud, all gashed and fretted with fire,
And the wind shrieked loud through his chamber, bellowing higher and higher,
And a knell as of death everlasting was knolled from a neighboring spire.

And the cloud rolled sulphurous into his brain, and the fire gnawed into his eyes,
And the tigerish wind whirled round and round, spiralling dervish-wise,
And tore into tatters the visual nerve, in its terrible fiery grind,—
And the steeple carillon lost its chime and tolled but the one word, "Blind!"

Well, it had happened ages ago, in the days that preceeded the flood,
So it seemed to Kyrle, with his strong hand lax and sluggish his galloping blood,

And over and over he cursed his fate and bitterly
marvelled to find
What a wretched contemptible thing is a man,
whether death-dumb and resigned,
Ox-like patient, stolidly mute, he draggeth his
weariful load,
Or furious snarls at the bloody lash and passionate writhes at the goad,—
Bah! the unstable frail spirit, more weak than
the wing of a dove
To soar and attain the empyreal heights,—strong
only to suffer and love!

Love,—to my story of love again, the wonderful
story we told
Or heard in the dim sweet cycles afar in the Age
of Gold,
When the pendulum pulse in the soft young
cheek swings tremulous to and fro
From the pearly pallor of cherry blooms to the
rose's crimson glow,
When a few faint syllables, English-plain, are
richer than wisdom's years,
And one dear voice holds deeper tones than the
music of all the spheres.

Scarce could one call it an interview between
these shadowy folk,

Whereof the one saw the other not and neither
the silence broke,
But at the third strange meeting-time, Kyrle
gathered courage and spoke,
For e'en as she laid her tribute down and would
have fled hurrying by,
He caught her hand in a deathful grip, unheed-
ing her startled cry,
Too wrapped in his infinite harrowing need, too
wholly absorbed to feel
The crusted wealth of her priceless rings, the
elegant sleeve of seal,
And he poured out his thanks in a sudden rush
as a brook doth in March overswell,
Entreating that she who had been but a fragrance
should now be a voice as well.

Long she stood hesitant, statue-still, her lilies
and fingers withdrawn,
And at last he sighed in a shuddering breath,
deeming she must have gone,
But then she answered and all the peace and
healing and balm that dwell
In a country lane on a Sabbath morn, blest by a
distant bell,
Hallowed her voice, and the words thereof were
sweeter than asphodel,

For pity, if pity she felt, was veiled under a sprightly essay
To twist a shimmering strand of gold into the hodden gray.

"Alas, poor knight! thou art lorn and lost, and cast forever away
In this enchanted and fearsome land, where witches and ogres hold sway,—
Thou hast suffered the ban of my sister Fate; but I am a tenderer fay,
And so that thou servest me early and late, owning no queen beside,
Never presuming to question my will, loyal whatever betide,
I dare avouch thou again shalt feel that warmly the sun doth shine,
Thou shalt once more breathe Heliconian air, and drink of Falernian wine,
And haply at last the scales shall fall fiom those dark sad eyes of thine!"

Then pressing the lilies close into his hand, while Kyrle stood blockish and still,
She murmured "Farewell, farewell, poor knight! Remember the Fairy Saville!"

IV.

TO WOMEN alone doth love, bright love, come as a perfect joy,
A lily uncankered, pure virgin gold, flawless and free from alloy,—
Faithfully, gladly they serve, who win, for tending the boy god's flame,
Guerdon of agonized travail and death and often a pilloried shame,—
They, sweet souls, do rapturous leap at the sound of Love's entering,
Ask not where he has hidden his lash, but worship and crown him king.

Men, it may be, have a loftier look, a glimpse of the anguish and tears,
And see in the baby's bassinette the corpse of seventy years,
The rift that must come in the lute at last, the worm that works in the bud,—
However it be, I only know their love is a vice in the blood,
A season of poignant tormenting, of pleasure elusive and vague,
A maelstrom engulfing, to be forever dreaded and shunned like the plague,—
To men, pink palpitant Eros seems a skeleton earthily gaunt,

And their kindest word for the fluttering shape
is "Horrible monster, avaunt!"

But when into Kyrle's existence blank, arid as
African sands,
Into the barrenness marred and vexed by alien
tongues and hands,
An angel's voice rang heavenly high, and a star
in his pathway fell,
Welcomer 'twas to the lonely man than water in
nethermost hell.
He troubled no more for his future weal than
violets do in May,
For steadily, softly gleamed the star; sufficient
from day to day
It was to hearken and ponder the words the
Fairy Saville would say,
Though ever he questioned his dubious heart,
"Can this great miracle be,—
Does this magnificent passion-flower blossom
alone for me?
Or hath she served an apprenticeship and gilded
her fancy's pen
Coldly dipping it, artisan-wise, in the blood of a
score of men?"—
But soon these petty misgivings fled,—what
mattered it if she had won

Her bountiful largess of healing under a fostering sun,
Or rooted on some bleak headland, torn by the mistral harsh,
Or midst of the drooping cypresses and beaded moss of a marsh,—
For she spoke not alone with the cold precision and icy glitter of thought,
That of itself no poetry forms, but all of her speech was wrought
With fluctuant gleams of the light divine that never on sea or land
Doth shine, but only in vestal hearts that tremble and understand,
And whether she struck with a touch assured the silver strings of her lyre,
Till the whole wood rang to a rhapsody as of a seraph choir,
Or whether she wailed in a minor key, sad as the coo of a dove,
Briny with tears as the ocean foam, a bitter-sweet story of love,
Or whether elegiac, organ-deep, she chanted a dirge-refrain,
Or of rivulets warbled and resinous buds and burgeon of meadow and plain,
Eloquent utterance, gracile as palms, poppies of fire and of dew,

Bloomed at his need like the manna of old, and
grateful he listened and knew
That God, who forbade him to read a poem, was
letting him live one through,
And his wing-clipt faith grew whole once more,
spurning its shackles and bars,
And he soared on pinions steady and strong to
the gracious accessible stars,
And man was honest and woman was true and
the Infinite God was kind,
And the world was a fair pure world again, and
only his eyes were blind,
And he bowed his head to the All-wise Will,
embracing the doom assigned.

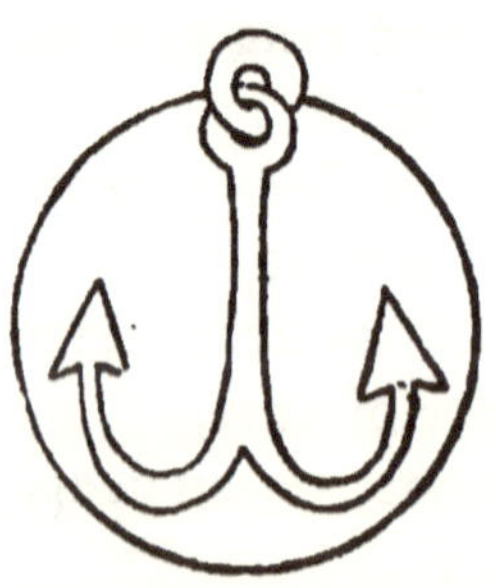

V.

WEEK after week slipped billowy by into
the gulfy past,
And the silvery beryl of each day's wave
broke at Kyrle's feet and upcast
Flotsam of Indian broideries, spices, and pearls
of Ceylon,
Sandalwood Araby sweet, and myrrh, and fagots
of cinnamon,
And strewing the sterile waste beach of his life
became as a godsend thereon.

The timid grace of the lady birch, the gnarls of
the oak, she told,
How the warrior pines stood stark against the
sunset's daffodil gold,
And the sinuous slopes of the distant hills were
but as a banner unscrolled,
Tawny and russet and purple twined, dotted with
orbs of jet
Where a sturdy thorn or a lichened rock was
into the fabric set,
And often she pictured a mother and babes, a
tranquil domestic scene
Behind the rubious cordial glow of a casement's
coppery sheen,
And once when the sky occidental was paly
translucentest green,

Like apple-tree buds ere the mid-May's kiss
quickens them, tender and keen,
She told how a trio of cloudy shapes, dripping
with blood and wine,
Drifted o'er the horizon's rim, lurid as almandine,
Huddled and hunched and wizened, like the sis-
ters three in Macbeth,
And one was Failure and one was Fear, and one
was a Prayer for death,—
But an airy knight pricked over the plain and
he vanquished them all at a breath,
And the conqueror's colors were caught and
tossed, and up to the zenith rolled,
And a legion sang of his victory like the morn-
ing stars of old.

And once she came through a shuddering storm,
braving the eddying whirl
Of the snow-grains sown by a prodigal hand,
and walked for a space with Kyrle,
And clung to his arm, half womanly guide, and
half but a frivolous girl,
And said 'twas as if they were walking alone,
they two, in a vast white pearl,
Where radiant nacre-gleams of pink traversed
the edelweiss hue,
But never a satyr's hoof was heard nor an
Oread's laugh rang through,

And there lurked no hint of the forestal green
nor yet of the limitless blue.

And then as they battled against the wind,
sauntering to and fro,
She preached him a little sermon she had studied
that day in Thoreau,
Her text, the chariot wheels of the storm, the
six-spoked crystals of snow,
Those faceted glorious spangles, the sweepings
of heaven's floor,
Feathery petaled hexagonal flowers, diamond
dusted o'er,—
Why, we are sprent with gems! they fall in a
wavering thistledown blur,
In the gallery of the meadow mouse, on the
restless squirrel's fur,
The schoolboy crushes them into a ball, the
woodman follows his sled
Through the wreck of a myriad fragile stars,
strange as the stars o'erhead,—
And Oh! 'twere a blasphemy to declare by some
cold narrowing word
Mechanical action got them: Divinity must have
stirred
In the germ pellucid and gelid, and so have they
come to be

Fair fruit of enthusiasm, the children of ecstasy,—
And mother nature not yet had lost her pristine vigór and force,
Still was the law supreme at work, the sun still true in his course,
And God still paused to watch over His earth, still fashioned with cunningest art
The baby flakes of the silver snow—and why should a man lose heart?

VI.

BUT at last came a day when she failed to come, when the reed bent rottenly down,
And he sat in a cruel impatience, his face deformed by a frown,
And he listened in vain for the crystalline tinkle of feet through the crepitant grass,
The delicate laugh of dismay at a drift or haply a tiny crevasse,—
He waited half sick of a hope deferred, till his marrow was turned to ice,
And the orange and garnet chilled out of the sky, and the lad had come for him thrice,
And then he arose and doggedly trudged to his poor pain-tenanted room,
That crawled as with slimiest horrors throughout the reticulate gloom,
And he shrank from shutting himself alone into that living tomb.

And he had no lilies at all that night, no languorous lullings of spice,
No hope of remote reparation, no visions to lure and entice,
Naught but the old, old Tantalus-mood, that had gathered new malice and gall
From disuse, as a robe gathers mildew and moth, hanging forgot on the wall,

And a pain rapacious surged over his soul like
a flood or a pestilent wind,
Or octopus-like sucked into his heart, shark-
toothed and poisonous-finned,
And he summoned the strength of his nature in
its outraged trust to arise
And help him to hate himself and this woman,
to utterly loathe and despise
Her who had made him a pastime, bridging the
winter across
With a masque, a foolery petty and vain, amus-
ing herself with his loss,—
God! it had been but an insult throughout, her
'havior so sisterly free,—
She scarce had esteemed him a man at all,—why,
then, forsooth! should she be
Distantly coy with a clod, reserved as a maid is
alway
With a man? She had seen at a glance that no
least possibility lay
Of love 'twixt herself and a creature ignoble, all
of whose manlihood
The chief enchanter had Merlin-wise sunk in a
pathless wood,
And so she had pitied him for a season, but now
she had wearied and sped
To a southern clime where the grapes were gold
and the pomegranates lusciously red.

But the Avon Swan sang silvery clear "All office infirmity still
Neglects," and his heart waxed weak and wailed "Perhaps she is fevered and ill,—
Perhaps she is dying—O God, protect Thy purest, Thy peerless Saville!"

Yet the foul faint doubt he had trampled at first sprang weedlike over again,—
She was but a woman and therefore false,—she smiled on a hundred men,—
And he thought how she clung to his arm in the snow and he wished he had killed her then!

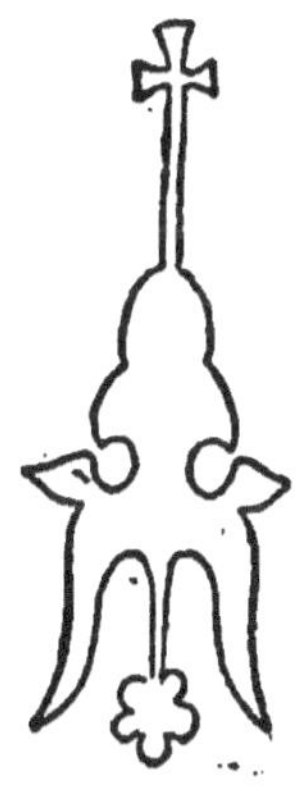

VII.

BUT the next day came, and with it Saville
too breathless and happy to speak,
And he felt the vibrant blood in her hand,
and he guessed it was red in her cheek,
And he said that he dared not reproach her—it
was not his right—and then poured
Upon her head meek and devoted such vials of
wrath as are stored
In a thunderbolt, wild over leaping the bounds
that convention hath set,
And Saville stood exultant and smiling to see
how a man could forget
All hindrances puny, external, and show forth
the soul of him yet.

But she stifled her smiling and gently spoke,
and there was a subtle change
In her tone and manner, a humbleness, sub-
servient, flattering, strange,
As when a poor peasant, gambolling rude, freely
will shout and sing
For a chance companion, but soon is hushed,
learning he rides with The King!

"I am sorry—yet glad—but sorry the most! I
never, I think, should have dared

To believe that my coming was aught to you,—
I deemed that you would not have cared,—
I might have ribboned a note to the bench,—
but alas! you could not read,—
And did you really linger till dark? and did you
miss me indeed?
But I—I was threading the tangled maze of the
city's ravenous whirl,
And I gazed for an hour upon 'Rupert's Trust,'
—and you, O friend! you are Kyrle!"

He mused, how small is the woman soul, how
timid and trustless and frail,
Curious ever of pedigree and trivial confirming
detail,
While he had not even requested her name, con-
tented as yet but to dream
Of her as a dim mist-maiden, a goddess, gem-
girdled, supreme,—
But it passed, this scornfulness fleeting, and the
air seemed to dimple and dirl
Eolian-tender, mandolin-sweet, at the magical
words, "You are Kyrle,"
Simple, sufficient, as if she had said in a homag-
ing, honeyfraught tone,
"You are Cæsar,—unmastered, unrivalled,—our
planet doth own

No man for your fellow,—Enough! You are even so Kyrle and alone!"

Ah, well! he had hoped that the world one day would thus acknowledge his power,
Would wreath his temples with immortelles, would cast at his feet the dower
That genius merits and sometimes wins; but alas! not e'en for an hour
Had he been the idol; the waxen bud had blackened and failed of a flower.
And now he inquired as a father might of a distant and darling child
Of the veriest trifles; he knew how hard they were to be reconciled,
The needs of a picture like "Rupert's Trust," and the mirk of a dusty shop,—
Was it decently hung? did the light fall true from a shaded jet at the top?
And Oh! was it verily great? did it hold the vital, the God-given spark
That had been his latest glimpse upon earth, that still struck white through the dark?
Was the flame still lambently blazing and clear, the gold from the dross to refine,
Of force to pierce and to purify men, and change then from panthers and swine?

Could a man step out of his daily round and that
passionate picture scan,
And not go forth to the greed and the grind a
cleaner and better man?
Had she heard as she gazed the Spirits of Good
singing their deathless song,
Had she felt it were better to starve and rot than
swerve to the smallest wrong?

But Saville was mute; it seemed for a space as
if she scarce could have heard,
She who was ever so prompt to utter a sparkling
felicitous word,
And he guessed she was weeping, and soon she
breathed in a tear-veiled tremulous tone,
"I only prayed: O God! Give back his vision
and take my own!"

And Kyrle laughed out, 'twas so sweet to win
compassion divine as this,
Laughed like a boy, and reached his arms over
the viewless abyss,
And the black was cleft by a lightning stroke
and their souls were fused in a kiss.

VIII.

AND as ever, the kiss to the maiden's lips came as a fleckless delight,
As a hummingbird glad in the amber noon recks never of tempest-torn night,
But the man thrilled solemnly to the thought that whether for good or for ill
He had mixed his life with another life and was bound as with steel to Saville,
And he raged at himself for an image of clay that senseless and selfish had snared
The love of a creature angelic, to whom he should never have dared
Lift even a worshiping thought, since his foiled adoration was but
As a rayless rare jewel, unmined, unprized, under a mountain shut.

Men take for granted the ferventest love; it seemeth them utterly meet
That woman should bow to them as to a god and lay at their deity's feet
Frankincense, honeycomb, turquois and pearl, and all things precious and sweet,—
But Kyrle, poor Kyrle, was humble enough, and he honestly questioned the maid
How she had formed so wretched a choice,—how had her fancy strayed

Past willowy wands and stalwart rods to the crookedest staff in the glade?
Her heart had bled for him, blind and banned, as any true woman's had done,—
He flung back her pity,—a goodly gift, mayhap; but he would have none.

Pity? no,—she was orphaned and sad; she dwelt in the hall of L'Estrange,
A mere companion and hanger on, forbidden to roam and to range
Past the walls of the park, lest her mistress should call, for she was capricious and strange,
And bitter as aloes her bread to Saville, who joyed as a bird to exchange
Her gilded dull cage for a wider bourne, her chrysalis wings to unfurl
In the ether of freedom and float for an hour in blessed communion with Kyrle.

"Ah sweet! for a rainbow hour 'twere well; but now you have tangled your life
With a pariah's, unto whom God denies the having of home or of wife."

"But dearest! that is the blazing star in this galaxy-bond of ours,

The regnant rose in a garland twined of sweet yet commoner flowers!
Thank God that the thought of marriage is as far as the thought of death,—
Marriage! where poor little weary Love, drabbled and out of breath,
Bravely struggles 'gainst pitiful odds, till his cruel coarse-spirited foes
Break and batter the irised wings and sneer at his dying throes,
And the dance and jest go rioting on, and none of his murdering knows!"

"Ah, well, I would risk it! but whether Saville, for us it could happen so,—
Perish the thought! 'tis a sacrilege,—but never, dear love, shall we know.
I am as a bee untimely crushed ere he unloadeth his sweets,
Dead to accomplishment, effort and joy, whose heart still cruelly beats,
Ardent, ambitious, and pulsing strong with fiery tropical heats,—
God! how I worship my art divine, my heavenly art, Saville,—
That I were rotting a grain a day, yet able to serve her still!"

Then Saville perceived what is common to all
who are linked with disciples of art,
That she stood without the holy of holies, an
alien, a stranger, apart,
But she passed the portal and coined a word to
comfort the desolate heart.

"Hearken, my dearest! You murmur because
you fancy you have not done
Your stent to the utmost, have painted but one
great picture,—but one!
You should rather thank God from a grateful
heart you were gifted to do so much,
For manifold millions of men go by, nor help
the world by a touch;
They loiter like lizards half frozen and maimed
over the face of the rock,
And they front their kind with no message more
true than a moan or a gibbering mock,—
But you! you are like to God in this, that out
of your innermost thought
You have created and called to life a thing with
deep potencies fraught,
And the work shall endure, inspiring and grand,
when the worker hath fallen to dust,
And my soul hath a loftier stature today for
looking on 'Rupert's Trust!'"

And he laughed once more. "Ah sweet, my sweet!
hath a nightingale lodged in thy breast,
That thou singest a strain more rapture-panged
than ever a siren possessed?
Yes, I have achieved—but ah! what I meant—
yet what are the claims of my art,
What joy had I won had I labored on like the
emperor's prize of thine heart,
That nest whence the doves fly gauzily forth
and the air with sweet flutterings fill,—
My darling, my darling! Yes, God is above,
and He loves me and sends me Saville!"

IX.

O FRIEND! if a brother, struggling and
faint, cries out for thy helping hand,
And begs for a draught of water or wine in
a barren and fountainless land,—
If a human soul in a need extreme where the
weltering surges roll
Entreats for a token of sympathy, the touch of
a stancher soul,
Hasten, O hasten to give of thy strength! let
not the poor sufferer wait,
For the sand burns white and the waves leap
fierce, and to-morrow it may be too late,—
Thou shalt haply see in the morning sun an
outworn shell at thy gate!

Saville had responded to Kyrle's wild prayer,
and so was permitted to save
His wounded faith and his breaking heart from
the dusty dark of the grave,
And the days like white-winged birds wheeled
by, and nearer and nearer they grew,
And each was a light in the other's life, tinging
its grayness through
With a cordial warmth, as in winter wolds ver-
milion barberries do,—
Ah me! 'tis a world of shadows we walk in, and
happy is he who can cling

In the midst of the vacillant spectres secure to
one real true thing.

And April arrived and the sward to the foot was
spongily tender and wet,
And the ice-bound brooks broke loose and ran
singing a canzonet,
And coral the maple-buds shone overhead, and
mayweed and thistles and dill
Were springing as if but to honor and please
sweet arbutus-laden Saville,
And Kyrle stood erect and majestic, awaiting
her, seeming again
Sovereign and lord of his turbulent fate, self-
poised and a man among men.

He had something to tell her—yet where was the
need? Her knowledge preceded his own—
She must have incited her lady L'Estrange, a
power behind the throne,—
The picture was sold to that lady,—no more
should it languish unseen,
But was called to its rightful station, the home
of a social queen,
And the lady had paid a liberal price, almost a
fabulous sum.
A monarch's fee, and 'twas through Saville that
this fortunate chance had come,

And so she had earned a commission,—she must
not be over nice,—
She was poorer than he himself was, and here
was the half of the price,—
He fathomed the dullness abhorred of her daily
routine at the Hall,
There were nettles 'mid silkiest cushions, and
the bread was besprinkled with gall,—
And here was the money, her earnings, not his;
she must take it and hasten away
To the rose-misted mountains or chrysoprase sea,
and rest for a long holiday.

One word incoherent and sudden she spoke in a
doubting reproachful tone,
Then struggled for dignity all too late, for the
word had been simply "Alone?"

Full often the mind, when fate's dense cloud
suddenly ominous lowers,
Or sparkles with gold or crimson, charged by
kindlier powers,
Works in the groove a master cut, in deeper ex-
pressions than ours,
And Kyrle but mused how the knight of old
mourned of his fateful sin

That he dare not pluck it forth of his heart, since all that was lovely therein
Was tendrilled and knotted with what was evil in union so vital and strong
That which was tainted and which was pure he wist not, nor right from wrong.

" Now surely this were a sin," mused Kyrle, "or a cowardice, which is worse,—
A month ago I had spurned the thought away from me with a curse.
What should such fellows as I do," forsooth? and Hamlet as good as his word,
Weak, irresolute, yet put by the plea of temptation unheard,—
Yes,—and thanks to his reasoning so unimpeachably sound,
To this Alpine glimmer of purpose high in his brain's fantastical round,
His poor, poor love with her pansied hands and her daisied tresses lay drowned!

And Oh! he was weary of prudence, that frigid fanatical nun,—
In her hateful name what straits he had seen, what tasks superhuman had done,

He had chidden his lips for smiling, forbidden
his blood to run,—
And now at the thought of breaking her bond,
Kyrle's heart, exuberant, wild,
Leapt as a cataract plunges o'er masses of granite
up-piled,—
Sweet is a reckless beat in a pulse long glacier-
gentle and mild!

Again did a master's words come back in rippling
mellifluous flow,
"Whither, O whither, my love, shall we flee for
a sweet little summer or so?"
And he said, "The thorn-girded Princess arose
and followed her lover,—but no!
You are hedged with a thousand conventional
briers, Saville, and you dare not go,—
It is but a dream that we twain might wed and
sweep in a swallow-like flight
Away for a roseate triple-mooned day, and then
ere autumnal sad night
Slip back to our niches appointed and strait,
and arm for the winter's fight,
Yours, the hushing of peevish complaints, the
filling of futile demands,
Mine, the patiently facing the dark and chafing
the listless hands,—

But no!—'tis the dream of a dastard, a dolt,—
'twere a children's folly, a sin—
Yet what right doing of all our lives, what sacrifice ever shall win
Reward so regal? And yet, the end! If I held
you once as a wife,
God! what a thing were I to sink content to the
old blank life!
But it is not I who shall blench at the risk,—
the madness, the crime, if you will,—
Yours is the right to rebuke or accede,—Will
you marry me then, Saville?"

Sobbing she answered, "Dear heart! the wrong,
if any there be is mine,—
I should have vision for both of us; but I am the
night-shade's vine,
Purple and scarlet with poison, throttling whatever I twine,—
These are hysterical ravings! Forget them!
My spirit hath passed
Through a long purgatorial penance, but now
soareth lark-like at last,
And I cannot be sorry this moment, dear heart,
e'en for your lampless eyes,—
I am glad they must fail to discern in my own
the exquisite rapture that lies

Mixed with my tears,—tears vanishing now under your kiss as the dew
In the sun! And where have you lingered, my king, these horrible centuries through,
While I pined and paled in the dungeon-damps, waiting for you—for you!"

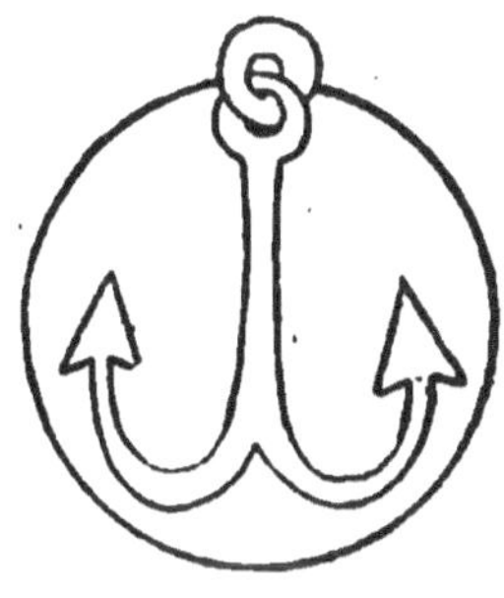

X.

O August imperial! Night divine! O infinite
passionate sea!
Each of itself is a gift so rich that well may
the high gods be
Envying man the sweet low earth and their beautiful trinity!

Kyrle and Saville went wandering on, slow pacing the surf-beat shore,
And he stumbled not, for she chose the path,
and heavy his arm hung o'er
Her delicate shoulders; so faithfully, so spaniel-humble she led,
Kyrle had not dashed his foot on a stone since
the vernal day they were wed.

Fair is the dawn, when the half-waked robins
closelier nestle and croon,
Fair, but faint by the smiting white supernal
splendor of noon,
And they who but warble of "Love's Young
Dream" methinks can never have known
The gordian tie of an older love, where shadow
and substance have grown
Incorporate utterly, not as the moss clings into
the crannied stone,

But knitted with intimate penetrant pangs, as
bone knitteth into bone,
By the hours when shuddering nature brings to
racking reluctant birth
Another soul to unravel anew the painful riddle
of earth,—
By the nights in the chamber of sickness when
the horror of death cleaves through,
And one fears to wipe or to leave unwiped the
brow of its clustering dew,—
By the time when the last hard gasp is hushed
and the poor little body lies still—
O God! I have not forgotten! Let any write
of it who will!
By the kisses that leaven the soddenest lives, the
kisses that stab as with spears
Of rapture the dull integument of the sordid and
leaden-paced years,
Kisses for which full many a man and maiden
have counted it well
To court dishonor and death and burn forever in
burning hell,—
Shall a slight thing come to dissever the twain
cemented thus heart to heart?
Shall they sundered be though earth divides?
Can God even drive them apart?

'Tis said that not overmuch do they speak, lovers long happily wed,—
Nay, 'twere superfluous,—where is the need? since all that the one would have said
The other discerns in a tangent tone, a sigh, or a lifted lash,
Whose hidden intent doth cycle and spread as the waves from a pebble's plash,—
But not as yet could this pair dispense with the word's mere pleasure and need,
Nor in silence commune, which accomplishment is a matter of lustrums indeed,
And Kyrle, sense-hampered and shorn of sight, delighted forever to hark
Saville, like Elaine, embroidering the velvety shield of the dark,—
She told how a race serenely pure dwelt in some fury-fed spark,
How a demon-brood infested the whitest orb of the glittering arc,—
How the wandering Pleiad was she herself, who had long, long ages ago
Resolved to dip to the dear dim earth, rocking so tiny below,
And had fearfully waited where comets whirred and planets loomed monstrous and grim,
Waiting the silvery summons of Love,—waiting for him, for him!

And she fretted oft at the noble verse of The
Book—"There shall be no night"—
For what were a day everlasting, garishly,
brazenly bright,
To this tablature soft and Egyptian, charactered
over with light,
Where the mind in the giant science trained,
the lore of the terrible stars,
Swings confident past the asteroids slight, past
neighboring Venus and Mars,
Out where each diamond grain of dust is a
throbbing and thousand-fold world,
And the intellect, steady and poised at first, is
faster and faster whirled
Till it staggers and swoons in the awful void,
and trembling and over-awed
Flies as a child to its father to the tenderer
thought of God.

And partly she worshiped the night because she
was liker her husband then,—
More than himself, she scarce could see,—the
star-seed, and now and again
A lamp in a cottage, a Stygian boat, and ever
the refluent line
Of the little sad waves that followed them, seeming to murmur and pine

And beg for an alms, a dole, from her too munificent share,—
She could weep in the midst of her happiness, hearing that endless prayer,—
There had been a time she had walked alone by the miserly sea, she said,
And for one pale pearl from its caverns dim herself had begged vainly instead;
She had woven a song, a trifling strain, of that starved and insatiate time,—
Would he hear the thing? she was something gifted, 'twas said, in music and rhyme.

ON THE BEACH.

The ocean is life and the beach
  Is time, and days are the waves
That heavily each over each,
  Now wild when the equinox raves,
Now languid in summer, do still
  Curl green with the coil of a snake,
And ponderous, cruel, and chill,
  In laughter and mockery break.

I hoped long ago that a wave
  Might bring to me jetsam of price,—
What tapestries silken and brave,
  What chests full of Indian spice
I fancied were destined for me

As I ran to and fro on the strand
In search of the treasures the sea
Must certainly bring to my hand.

But thousands of waves have come in,
Mere bubbles and foam as their freight,—
Oh, weary the watching has been,
And still do I hungrily wait,
For what? for a morsel of bread,
Though scarce if it comes within reach
Can I rouse from this apathy dead,
So famished I wait on the beach!

And Kyrle mused silent, while slowly his mind, as whelmed in the gulf-stream's drift,
Swirled far in a vague speculation: This poetic, this perilous gift,
Whose owner may dwell in the ultimate stars and is free of a fairy-knoll,
Who heareth the grass give thanks to the rain, who readeth a dragon-fly's soul,
Who trembles at night to list the winds conspire and whisper and plot,
Who of choice is blind to all false foul things and seeth but that which is not,
How can a creature like this endure humanity's sordid lot—
How sink from its rosy and opal haunts in filmy Elysian tracts

To life and its commoner uses, its hard mathematical facts?

That song of Saville's—she had suffered, be sure; one could hearken the ruddy slow drip
From a heart which relentless Fate had crushed in mortal implacable grip,—
Ah, well! we are born to suffer,—we are bound in an iron spiked wheel
And roll down a slope precipitous till the senses sicken and reel,
And haply their sorrows are lighter and less who can sing what their fellows but feel!

"Thanks for your song, my sweet," he said "it quickens and quivers with truth,—
And yet I must marvel a woman like you, dowered with beauty and youth,
Should have girded at loneliness blank yet brief, nor have guessed it was certain to end,—
Did you not know God in His own good time would happy deliverance send?"

The liquid plaint of the lapsing waves was the only sound for a space,
Then Saville: "My beauty you never have named till now,—shall I dexterous trace

Word-semblance thereof, and limn for you the
lines of this poor fair face?"

"Not so!" laughed Kyrle, "too well I fathom
your woman's and poet's ways—
The truth within you abideth not,—you would
lure me into a maze,
And muddy your matchless beauty, miring it
with dispraise!"

"No, no!" quoth Saville, "Oh, I should not
dare!—What, speak of my person a lie,
Defaming the charms which had you but seen I
surely had won you by?
Nay, dear heart, shall I paint for you a meteor's
arrowy flight,
The captain jewels that blaze serene in the tiara
of night,
And not do justice to this my beauty and bring
it full plain to your sight?
For I am beautiful,—amethyst clear are mine
eyes, and yet amaranth deep,
Violets held by a nixie's hand under the liquid
sweep
Of a brook, little wells where truth celestial lieth
in summery sleep,
And my hair glints gold as our marriage ring,
and lifts in a shimmering cloud

Over a face that is girlish fair, candid and noble-
browed,
Yet 'ware of its own perfections high, and something haughty and proud,
Scarce warmer in tint than the cornel's leaf or a
runlet's eddying foam
Till your voice or touch calls the straying blood
back to its natural home,
And then,—not the heart of a half-blown rose
holds ever a hue so sweet
As the pink in the cheek of a woman where
youth and happiness meet!"

"I am as a wanton boy who rifles the trillium's
marshy bed,
And wins unweeting an orchid rare, sacred,
dove-shapen instead,—
I, presumptuous, kneel at your shrine, abasing
my penitent head!"

"Yet what is Beauty unknown of Love? Naught
but a sea-lamp unfed,
Uninformed by the golden oil and flame, a dark
in the dark overhead,
No beacon to save the mariner's bones from
seeking the bones of the dead,—
And I was not always so beautiful, dear; the
flush and the light to my face

Came as the sun strikes rosily through some
cold alabastrian vase
With the first swift words that I heard you say,
and 'twas under your quickening kiss
That I grew to be as adorable, love, as parian-
perfect as this!"

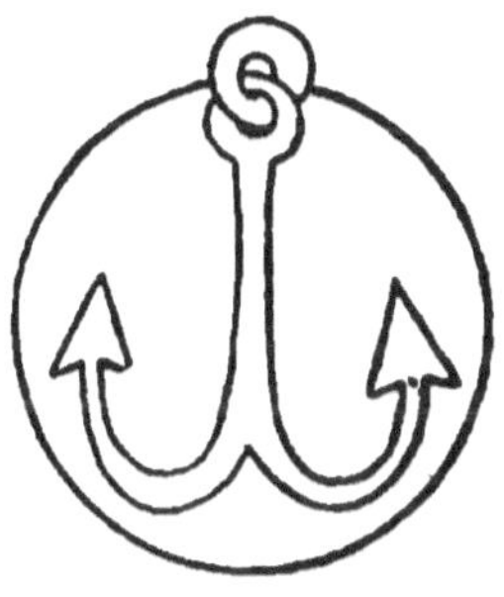

XI.

CAME a season when Nature from smiling ceased and lay with a deathstruck stare
Drowned on the beach with oozy weeds and brown wet shells in her hair,
With her vesture drenched and her poor bruised feet lying all stark and bare,
And leviathan billows bemocked their prey, and mangled and mouthed her there.

And the wind demoniac howled around the house, scarce more than a hut,
Where Kyrle and Saville and their happiness were safe from the tempest shut,
And the cheery lamp shed a kindly glow over the humble place,
And the nets and the bits of coral and spar lent it a simple grace.

" If only this cottage were ours, Saville! if this our idyl might be
Played for a white half-year divine down by the ice fringed sea!
But alas! the sable curtain must drop, and the actors perforce must flee!"

Then the wife, who crouched on the rug, her head on her husband's knee,

Murmured, "Fret not thyself, dear heart, but
leave thou the matter to me!"

"No, no!" said Kyrle, "you have often read
how shipwrecked men in a boat
Of their meagre provision of water and bread
take painfullest reckoning note,—
Sweet captain, how many days shall elapse that
we together may float?"

Then the woman broke out in a passion of sobs,
grovelling down on the floor,
"Oh, I have tricked you and trapped you, Kyrle!
I am vile to the innermost core!
I am not what I seem—what I swore that I was,
to make your deception complete,
A destitute girl,—I am rich instead,—rich, and
a liar and cheat!"

Then Kyrle sprang up in an agonized whirl of
righteous horror and wrath,
Like one who beholds a malignant snake rear
green and gold in his path,—
What! had he given his father's name, his heart,
and his honest clean hand
To a thing defiled by the pavement's soil, out of
society banned,

Destined to uses unlawful and stamped with a scarlet brand?
Not oft in this century's languid end do the fingers itch to garrote
Like the Moor's the blue-veined animate snow of a darling delicate throat,—
No, no! 'twas a virginal soul, Saville's,—the eyes of his mind were not seared,
And his heart fell calm and he said "Speak on!" and she never wist what he had feared.

Then she told her story,—how she herself was the beautiful chatelaine
Of L'Estrange,—how her wealth and beauty were tawdriest baubles and vain,
For of all the suitors that asked her hand never a one could convince
The maid that he wooed for herself alone, a genuine Fairy Prince,
And then when he came in triumph at last, her hero, her king, her Kyrle,
And offered his tiny pittance as to a dowerless girl,
What could she do but accept it and dwell with him down by the sea
In a world where romance and passion and bygone miracles be?

How she had panted to tell him! her heart had
ached that a lie,
However so harmless and tacit a one, should
sully their intercourse high,
That a gossamer slight as a thistle's down should
cross the cerulean sky—
There were wives, she knew, who smiled and
sang, some sepulchre-secret untold—
She herself was a verier woman than such, nor
cast in an Amazon-mold,
And now that he knew her trespass a weight
from her bosom rolled!

Kyrle silent sat, but he reached his hand to the
living gold of her hair,
Thinking how pure must the nature be, how in-
wardly white and fair,
That cowered at such a venial sin in uttermost
shame and despair,—
Their bond, though of steel, had unriveted been;
most perfectly had she known
They must travel their weary and several ways,
walking forever alone,
If but to his spirit startled and proud a hint of
the truth were blown,—
She had had wisdom and daring for both—Ay,
she had been overwise!

A serpentish feminine creature, compounded of
 lures and of lies,
Void of the commonest honesty even, false to his
 helpless eyes,—
Strange! that tonight, next week, next month,
 or when fifty years had gone by,
Whether she chid or caressed him or laughed,
 or mourned with a bitter sad cry,
He perforce must debate the thing in his heart,
 "But is this true now, or a lie?"—
Why, he had trusted her as his God, and lo!
 she had bought him and sold,
Made him a chattel, a page, a toy to deck with
 her chains of gold,
A Delilah's dupe,—'twere better to be mould in
 the churchyard mould!

Ah, well! myself, I have pity alone for the
 women who fail of the right,—
I know not in faith how it is we are made so the
 black seemeth often the white,—
We aspire to a dew-drop's clarity, to a resolute
 self-control,
To face the world—why, the woman lives not
 who even can face her own soul!
Ah, frail is our tenure of sanity, safety, serenity,
 calm,

At the mercy of any unlooked-for pang or merest material qualm,
And the astral truth that is grasped today in prayerful solitude
Seems but a trifle, a thing of naught, in tomorrow's hysterical mood!

But Kyrle was a man and so heaven had blessed him with absolute masculine sense
Of the right and the wrong, with a grand disdain of subterfuge and pretense,—
He had harbored a foe in his household, and now he was stung with a doubt
How to punish the viperish evil and cast the intruder out.

Then Saville, still sobbing, writhed up to her knees, and he felt her poor heart beating wild
'Gainst his own, resentful and harsh as Lear's, obdurate, unreconciled,
And for pity she plead, and pardon, and her plea was the plea of a child,
"There are many worse women than I am, dear,—truly, though you have forgot,—
I must read you the terrible papers and show you if there are not!"

And she seemed of an infantine weakness, and
sudden he felt ashamed
To be wroth with so cyclamen-frail a thing, and
never a word he blamed
His penitent love, but hushed her sobs, imploring her not to weep,—
And she strove with a broken smile to obey; but
thrice in the midnight deep,
Kyrle, lying awake while the equinox raged,
heard a moan break sharp through her
sleep.

Ah! in that night that must come to us all, when
a dear one low lies in the grave,
Pray God that we need not remember how once
the lost darling did crave
In vain for our word of forgiveness and tenderest
patience,—Nay, more!
Pray God we recall some moment we might justly
have scarified o'er
With lava-reproaches a trembling offender, but
sweetly forbore!

XII.

OUR life is a triplicate twisted cord of gray
and of gold and of white,—
The gray is the strand of the body and sensuous subtle delight,
The gold is the intellectual force, Jovian in triumph and might,
And the essence astatic, ethereal, eternal, that is
the filament white,—
And none on the low brown earth there be so
wholly of white and gold,
So rapt in unperishing verities on heights of
Siberian cold,
So saturate with conviction, so pierced with
truth icicle-keen,
As to cast the servitude utterly off of pleasure
in things terrene,—
And Kyrle, lapped soft in a luxury he never
had known or had dreamed,
Grew half content for a little space with the
things of this world and seemed
To drowse in uxorious slothful fields, lotosed,
Lethean-streamed.

And Saville was the sweetest of ministrants; the
scheme of her life was full plain
To her sight; she but lived for this man; her
fathers had garnered the grain

Of their wealth for his use and behoof; her mother had travailed and died
That Kyrle in the fullness of time might have her to hold as a bride,—
She had studied the lore of the ages, had drawn from Pierian wells,
Her fingers and voice she had trained to blend as the pealing of silver bells,
She had learned to wile from the poet's page a poetry more than his own,
Had won from the spinning earth its song and its axle's undertone,
Merely that he in his barred black cell might feel himself less alone.

We can but smile at the modern cry for an equaler social plan,—
Man is the servant of God alone, but woman serves God and man,
And God is the greater, certainly, but man dwelleth here below,
Not at a vast vague altitude, too loftily far to know
If we lay at his altar the homage meek, the allegiance that we owe.
We may wrap in a napkin our talents and God will not thunder or smite,

But woe to the household drudge who keepeth
the fire on the hearth not bright.
What are we in spite of our gifts and graces but
merest Circassian slaves
Shallops fragile or stately ships lashed by the
wind and the waves,—
And none dare impugn though the ocean be
covered with rudder-less spume-sprent
wrecks,—
'Tis nature's immutable law, and endures through
the ages while sex is sex.

———

I grant we might wander in wisdom's ways and
follow the windings thereof,
If we might but free our little white feet from
the tangling briony, love,—
'Tis sad when a woman to whom the fates Antony's
powers allot
Will eloquent thrill a multitude, for freedom will
plan and will plot,
Then weeps next morning a good two hours for
a parting kiss forgot!

———

Yes, truly,—'tis said there are women who their
earthly pilgrimage run
Unloved, unloving as is the Sphinx; speak not
of it; me, I am one

With a horror of any monstrosity rank in the
smile of the sun!

But to resume: This lesson, O friend, God
grant thou hast long ago learned,—
No blossom that springs in our weedy path is
small enough to be spurned,—
Is it a gold-graven chalice of wine, the cup of
thy present delight,
Or only an oak-leaf filled from a spring, dripping
with diamonds white?
Drink thou as if it were proffered of gods, e'en
as the draught were thy last,—
To-morrow mayhap the water and wine and the
sweet strong thirst will have passed!

Came a day when Saville saw 'twas over, saw it
too cruelly plain,
The months that had been a restoring lull 'twixt
gusts of repining and pain,
As an eglantine scent blown over a brook 'mid
dashes of August rain,
As the noontide rest of two wayworn gipsies hid
in a leafy lane,—
For seeking out Kyrle in his room one day she
found him asleep in a chair,
The westering rays on his handsome face and
bronzing the brown of his hair,

And he seemed as a carven statue, and the wife
stopped stricken and gasped,
For close in his long unused right hand his
palette and brushes were grasped.

And how he had found in the dark these things
she could not imagine or know,
And she closed the door and stole away, leaving
him sleeping so,
And in solitude knelt for a bitter hour and
wrestled alone with her woe,
Yet loved him a hundred-fold better because he
had broken the thrall
Of her arms for a vision of duty, nor made her
his all in all.

Came another day,—outside 'twas wild, and the
wind whistled scimetar shrill,
Whipping the terrified snowflakes sheeplike
over the hill,
But in the library dense with thought where
loitered Kyrle and Saville
Peaceful was all the atmosphere, solemnly, heavenly still,
Save as the woodbine tapped the pane with little
coquettish starts,
Or an ash fell feathery on the hearth 'neath
rosy and violet darts.

They were sitting the width of the room apart
and she had been reading from "Maud,"
When sudden he spoke in a voice at once exultant and deeply awed,
"Saville,—dear heart! I have not dared to say
what for days I have guessed—
That God in His infinite mercy and wisdom and
love accounteth it best
To relume the lamps in their sockets, to summon the long-fled guest,
To roll the hideous weight away that years on
my life hath pressed,—
There, as I point, is a grayness—a glimmer—a
dark less Cimmerian profound,—
Am I right? Is it haply a glimpse through a curtainless casement of snow-covered ground?
Here on the left is a lurid lifting of shadow,—it
almost is red,—
Is it only a sulphurous devil within, or the
ruddy clear fire instead?
I scarcely dare hope,—yet I have remembered
all of this year, Saville,
That the day we met you promised my sight—
But what is it, love? Are you ill—
Are you gone from the room that I meet with
alone this silence so strange and so chill?
Why, I looked for a tempest of laughter and
doubts, and for floods of rejoicing tears,—

We shall never have cause for such joy again in
all of our three score years!
Speak, I command you! 'Tis cruel as hell to
mock at my helplessness so,—
'Tis unworthy, unwomanly, all unlike the tender
Saville I know,—
Dear, I am frightened—a whimpering child—
come to me or I go
Seeking you, sick to the soul with fear, stagger-
ing to and fro!"

And he rose and gropingly crossed the room,
grasping the empty air,
And loud in his heart was a knocking dread and
low on his lips was a prayer,
And at last by the door his foot struck dull in
the coil of her soft sweet hair.

XIII.

THE pulse came back to the marble wrist and the faint sad lids unfurled,
And Saville perceived with a wild regret that 'twas not the end of the world,
And slowly she turned on her languid divan, dismissing them all from the room,
And shuddering flung her cerements off, like Lazarus in the tomb,
And dragged her rebellious feet across the velvety carpet, and flung
Herself odalisque-wise on a couch where a mirror magnificent hung.

For women, methinks that the text should read, "If haply ye have all things
And have not beauty, then have ye naught," for beauty such benison brings
No woman would barter it for a crown or the wealth barbaric of kings!
Ah me! we are gambling our lives away, playing a desperate game
Where we suffer in winning or losing alike,—'tis law, and there's no one to blame,—
And the stake that we play for is only love, and beauty and love are the same,
Or if not the same, then so closely knit that none can dissever the two,—

Men swear that they love us for mind or soul, and haply they think they do,
But the veriest dairymaid milking her cow knows it is wholly untrue;
Surely, plain women are sometimes loved; but Love is a wizard so kind
That he glamours and gilds the thing beloved, and causeth his servant to find
In his choice the graces of Hebe, Minerva, and Venus combined!

O friend! think never to please a woman by praising her housewife's thrift,
Her spiritual fervor and zeal for God, her rythmic or musical gift,—
Say rather you like the shape of the ear, or the eyelid's languorous lift!

Saville was enwrapped in a silken robe, woven of delicate pink,
All branched with lilies of silver, petalling link into link,
Fair as the blush of the peach in May, and silver and pink were her feet,
And her body was framed of a lily's curves, silverly white and sweet,
And her hair was a glimmering golden mist, the aureole of a saint,

A heavenly halo above a face—Nay hush! for I
dare not paint
That face with its birthmark fatal and foul, its
hideous carrion-taint!

But Saville had confronted it all her life, and to-
day with a ghastly mirth
She twisted her lips to a livid smile, "'Tis well
that she died at my birth,
My mother," she mused, "for to-day her life she
would deem but of slenderest worth!"

And she lay and mourned how strange it was,
how passing all utterance sad
That naught in the heart or mind of a woman
the love of a man forbade
So utterly as a surface blemish, a faulture gossamer thin,
Sprung from a tissue freighted too deep or a
hindered current within,—
For a woman may have a petrified heart, icy,
and rock to the core,
Scarred by tempests and seamed and gashed,
lichened and rusted o'er,
Of pity incapable, never to beat with a pulse of
kindliness more,—
She may have a mind, if you call it a mind, the
sluggish dull animal sense

That biddeth her eat and cover her limbs and
maketh a decent pretense
To veil with chatter or shroud with silence the
shame of her ignorance dense,—
She may have a lupine and viperish soul, disin-
tegrate with disease,
Fibrous and pulpy with poison, a pestilence
spoiling the breeze,—
'Tis a pitiful comment on this our life that a
woman may have all these,
And yet for her royal favor a man will sue on
his knees,
Dazzled so blind by her beautiful face that
never a fault he sees!

If ever a woman on earth might hope to be wor-
shipped for mind alone,
Or heart or soul, 'twas Saville, who was worthy
the love of a prince to have known,—
But ah! 'tis impossible—nature revolts—men
may sin against God on high,
But not 'gainst the law of selection; however
they truckle and lie
And successfully feign, they cannot love a thing
from which love must fly,—
Poor girl! she had seen in pauper's hovels where
she was dispensing bread

Disgust in the eyes she had wiped of their tears,
  a sneer on the lips she had fed,
A beggar's brat full patient and still through
  many a fevered dream
Yet start convulsive at sight of her face and turn
  with a ringing scream,—
She had come to believe that the dogs in the
  street howled as she passed them by,
And every glance at her face was a blow, and
  her every breath was a cry!

And now her body seemed but as a leaf that
  shrivels and curls in a flame,
And she shrank as a slave shrinks under the
  whip under her terrible shame,—
She had given herself as a wedded wife to a
  stainless knight and a true,
She whom never a churl on earth could know-
  ingly, honestly woo,—
Oh! in a biting shame like this there's only one
  thing to do!

Ah, why did he love her so passing well? For
  the very force of that love
Idealized, glorified, sanctified her, throned her
  all women above,
Made her a star in the firmanent, the marvel and
  wonder thereof,—

He thought to see if at last he awoke from his two years' visionless trance
That she whom the fates had sent to him by a miracle's happy chance
Was a goddess unparagoned, cinctured with cloud, divinely, immortally fair,
Sceptred and crowned with loveliness, a nimbus upon her hair,
Violets springing up under her feet—O God! O God! could she dare
Lift her Medusa-face to his own and harden it into despair?
A commoner, coarser-natured man might better have borne such blow,
But Kyrle to be gyved to this body of death,—Kyrle to be manacled so,—
Kyrle, with his artist's vision for colors and contours trained,—
Kyrle, forsooth! And she laughed aloud, seeing what thing remained!

And 'twas not the physical stigma, the blot on the skin alone,—
That his spirit might soar above,—but Oh! he could never condone
Her wicked deceit of silence, her garbled superfluous lies,

That were as a snivelling hypocrite's prayers,
a whining coward's who tries
To slaver himself with pretense of virtue and
whiten him in God's eyes!

A sound behind her, and Kyrle came in, and with
her low call for a guide
He crossed the room with his slow soft step and
sank on the couch at her side,
And belted her body within his embrace and
pressed his clear ivory cheek
'Gainst hers—no, not that word—no, no! but
barred with its baleful streak,
And murmured, "Saville, my wife, my queen—
pardon the haste that could speak
Such tidings so blunt—'twas a glowing breeze
and thou but a hyacinth weak,—
And hast thou a womanish fancy, love, that
mayhap we might drift apart,
I having once more the armor and steed to enter
the tourney of art,—
That I might grow careless of home and thee?
Perish the thought, sweetheart!
There's one fair thing in the world, Saville, that
ever I long to limn,
That first shall dawn on my long, long dark and
rise through the shadows dim,

That is more than the emerald forests or azurine heavens to me,
For a mother ne'er longed for her babe unborn as I this treasure to see,
Which is mine and still not mine as yet,—thou knowest it? thou canst guess?"

And Saville, with her eyes on the mirror, steadily answered "Yes!"

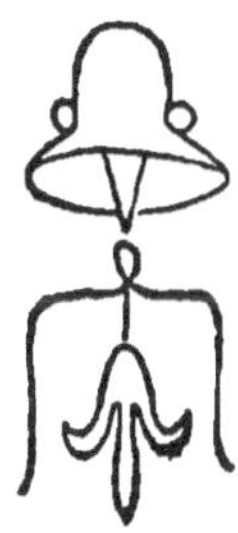

XIV.

WE MAY dwell content in a lowly cot,
wearing our homespun gray,
Neighbored by robins and lambs alone
and the squirrels across the way,
Disprizing wealth and keeping aloof from the
breakneck race of greed,
Our brows unbeaded by hard-wrung sweat; but
in time of a dear one's need
Money is freedom, 'tis wings, 'tis power, 'tis
verily life indeed,—
Oft do we watch our darlings droop in the merci-
less Northern blast
Knowing we well might save them if fortune
would only cast
In our way the means to carry them far where
zephyrs auroral blow—
What the rich spend oft in a single feast—if only
'twere ours—but no!
'Tis ours instead to watch next spring the grass
on a new grave grow!

Saville herself wrote bravely the letters sum-
moning over the land
The skill that hath earned the right to come at
only a Crœsus' command,
And she quietly waited the verdict; she had
written with steady hand

And heard with uneager impassive face the words
 of the surgeon bland:
There was every warrant for deeming the eye-
 balls' nubilous blur
A mere superficial obstruction; he would confident even aver
They should see complete restoration; and Saville gave sign of no stir
In her pulse at this gospel of light to him, of
 dark everlasting to her,
And never her fingers faltered through many a
 day and night
To bathe with lustral lotions and to number the
 drops aright.

And as one death-doomed by a mortal ill, knowing his sojourn is brief,
Wastes never the precious moments in useless
 repining and grief,
But rather endeavors to sweeten each hour, to
 make its scarce-hoped-for boon
Something to sweetly recall 'mid the dark he
 reluctant must enter so soon,
So Saville grudged every atom of time she did
 not with Kyrle commune.

She little had practiced the ways of the world,
 this cloistered immured Saville,

But now she set snares for the bird Renown, and the journals began to fill
With notes of Kyrle's long hid sketches, praise of his wonderful skill,
Predictions of his renascence and greater triumphs in store,
So that he gleefully laughed as she read, reminding her o'er and o'er
How she had said in her very first words that if he would only adore
The Fairy Saville all things of good would serfs at his beckoning be,
"And first 'twas Love and then 'twas Wealth, dear heart, that thou gavest me,
And now 'tis Fame, and Vision draws nigh, lured to mine eyes by thee!"

And he said 'twas strange to reflect indeed that if he had been alone
Throughout the term of his blindness, if God had not made her known
To his cankered heart, 'twas certain the mordant malevolent tone
Of his mind would have tainted his later life, projecting through future days
When the hand's sleight wedded to strength of purpose should fill the world with his praise,

And had marred his work with an atheist's doubt
of God and His questionless ways.

But e'en as he strayed, a bewildered child, where
the tide swirled over the beach,
A starry seraph had caught his hand and guided
him safe out of reach
Of the waves seductive of unbelief and their low
insidious speech,
Whispering, "God is over us all, and He cares
for His children each!"

And he said that often it frightful seemed that
aught should hinder or ban
Our life of a minute's duration, should shorten
the firefly span
Of effort and strength and passionate zeal for
truth allotted to man,—
But it had been well for himself to pause,—in
the interval he had thought,
Had won experience deep and rich that should
in his work be wrought,
And he could not thank her in all his life for the
wonderful things she had taught,—
Henceforth his pictures should sing of her, Saville
their dominant tone,
Merely the pigments and tactile skill, the outward
shell, were his own,

While the essence informing, the spirit divine,
that was Saville's alone!

And he had fought down his impious wish:
Though helped by Angelico's shade
To worthily trace her portrait, he was certain
that if he essayed
So high a task great Jove would smite and the
thunderbolts make him afraid!

XV.

EACH century hath, it is said, its peculiar favorite sin,
A chamber of horrors so grewsome and dank no poet may dwell therein,
But the special crime of this passing day touches us all so near
We cannot therefrom withdraw our eyes however they widen with fear,—
The journals will spare no details of the suicide's act and its cause,
The plunge or the bane or the bullet—Why may not the people have laws
To defend them from hearing these blasts of hell? O tribunes and senators! pause
In your framing dispensable edicts, smoothing scarce-visible flaws,
And forbid the monsters black-blooded and huge to mangle these gouts in their maws!

Saville heard her sentence of death, she felt, in hearing the surgeon say
The bandage should fall and the curtains be drawn on the first sweet morning of May,
A year ago—how the robins had sung!—it had been their wedding day!

When instinct of self-preservation is nulled and
"life maddens 'gainst life amain,"
The very loss of that chief instinct is proof of a
clot on the brain,
And it eats and honeycombs night and day like
a burrowing mole in the ground,
Whether one dances or dines or sleeps, till a vital point it hath found,
And the deadliest sting of the subtle disease, the
devil's insidious touch
Is that though a temptation to mortal sin one
knoweth it never for such,
But esteems it the highest duty to which a soul
can aspire,
And is lighted to self-destruction by the martyr's
sacrific white fire,—
And how shall one fail to follow where the im-
molate saints have trod,
How shrink from inflicting upon one's self the
flagellant's merited rod,
How fear to cast out mere offal—a burden so little worth
There no longer is room for it anywhere in all
of the sweet wide earth?

Look you,—why, haply beneath your roof one
weareth a steady smile,

Sedately pacing life's minuet, while steadily all
the while
A horrid design is forming, a fungus spreads
cancerous-vile,—
I have held the hand of a friend one hour and
the next his spirit had fled,
Dismissed by self and violent means—Who
knows? Had I sisterly said
A word of love I might have dissolved and
melted his purpose dread,—
Clasp close the near ones about your hearth, let
never caresses lack,
For the turn of a card, the fall of a leaf, may
speed them adown the track
Facile, declivitous, into the bourne of the
Acheron valley black!

Yet no,—this were not of the least avail; no aid
that is won from without
Is of force to cope with interior foes, to vanquish
and put them to rout,—
The brood ignoble and self-engendered must
even self-stifled be,
For a wanton zephyr deracinates not the stur-
diest forest tree,
And often this deadly virus breeds in a strong
determinate mind,

In a soul more stalwart and loftier far than the bulk of the human kind,
Whose motive is not a coward's, to spare itself woe and disgrace,
But to rid the world of a tainted thing, to die for the sake of the race.

Yet if so be that one conquers temptation and out of the gates of hell
Flame-blackened with shrivelling garments back cometh alive and well,
There's not on the earth a stronger soul than such a king-spirit must be,
That hath even outdaunted Satan himself, bidding him tremble and flee,—
Nothing can shake the integrity, the rock's impregnable strength
Of the fort long assaulted that now is left to its hard won peace at length,—
Exalted, serene, the spirit shall reign in its untouched citadel,
And look henceforth with an equal eye on the things of heaven or hell;
Less ineffable now is the heliotrope scent, and life seemeth scarcely so sweet,
But neither looms death so dragonish grim nor annihilate dark so complete,

For the soul that was but as a reed in the wind
hath attained a Nirvana of calm,
And is in this feverous desert of life a fountain
of healing and balm,
And pilgrims shall be refreshed thereat, shall
gratefully lave and drink,
And maidens shall garlands wreathe of forget-
me-nots fringing the brink,
And many shall love the spring fern-hidden,
shall precious esteem it and dear,
Not knowing what throes volcanic and fierce
have left it so crystalline clear.

XVI.

SWEET April, blossomy April, the laughing capricious maid,
Had velvet enamellar carpets spread in garden and glebe and glade,
Had carelessly dropped her loose-clasped gold, dotting with coins the lawn,
Had lingered for thirty ravishing days, and to-night was almost gone,
For the latest even of April had come, and the soft air, moist with rain,
Stole through the ivied casement, a lilac breath in its train,
Over the two who had known together a year of divinest love,
And who now had come by the will of fate to the last sweet moment thereof.

" Kyrle, I have something to ask," she said, timidly stroking his hand,
" Answer me not with blame of my weakness, but try, dear, to understand,—
It is that you let me leave home to-night,—but of course, dear Kyrle, not for long,—
I dare not be present to-morrow,—I have aye been so brave and so strong
That haply you think I can bear all things,—but if the result should go wrong,

If you should not see as they say you will, if instead of triumphal song,
Your voice breaks down in a heartstruck wail at a failure abrupt and complete,
I could not survive the cruel shock,—I should drop down dead at your feet!"

"Nay now, Saville, thou art far too bold,—why, what shall it profit me
The fleecy flocks of the sky to mark, the crocus and primrose to see,
Ay, even my first love, 'Rupert's Trust,' and not—O Saville! not thee?
Yet thou shalt never ask boon in vain,—I will thine almoner be,
A warden most lenient,—Go, dear heart! for a score of hours thou art free!"

And softly she thanked her lord and liege, meek as a scriptural wife,
And he might not discern from her even tones with what pangs her bosom was rife,
Nor dreamed that in passing away that night she was passing sheer out of his life.

And she came and knelt by his chair once more, wrapped in her soft rich cloak,

And nestled her poor sad face in his breast and brokenly, tenderly spoke,
" O love, my love, in the days to come winnow thy mind of the ill
I haply have done thee,—remember alone that I was thy Fairy Saville! "

And he kissed her thrice and he said "Good-night," and she bit back a passionate cry,
And he noted not in his hope and joy that her answering word was " Good-bye! "

XVII.

IT WAS over, his long suspense and doubt; the delicate daring hand
Had executed successfully the intellect's keen command,—
O, scarce in the New Jerusalem paven with gold and with pearls,
Scarce shall the ransomed of God know rapture diviner than Kyrle's!

For an hour or twain 'twas enough to enjoy, merely that God had said
"Let there be light!" for him once more, and had summoned his eyes from the dead,
But quickly the rift crept widening in,—'twas but a mere broken toy,
A splintered gem, a goblet cracked, if Saville did not share in his joy.
He blamed himself for granting her prayer,—she should have remained beside
Her husband and bravely fronted with him what weal or woe should betide,—
Alone? Why, not so alone had he been before they ever had met,—
A tenebrous wall of solitude, carven of solid jet,
Immured him round, and the air waxed cold, e'en as the sun had set.

He sought the room where her laugh and song had made the obscurity bright,
And gazed on trifles familiar and dear to the touch if not to the sight,—
Her bird chirped low in its shining cage, the fish gleamed gay in the globe,
And careless it lay on the rich divan, her rosy and silvery robe,—
Yes, she herself would be here anon—where else should she be?—but yet—
Surely the hour was passing—had passed—the hour she had set
To return—Good God! he was stifling, meshed in a strangling net!

They brought him a note. "Dear Kyrle, Dear Love, Briefly and plain must I write,
Nor tax God's last best gift to you, the peerless blessing of sight,—
They who shall give you this letter will tell you wherefore it must be
That you and I are severed nor meet till we meet by the jasper sea.
I had meant to leave you another way,—but I could not! my aim would have missed
The head that your hands had benisoned, the bosom your lips had kissed,—

I could wish 'twere a loftier motive, dear, some
 impulse of duty or right,
But no,—'twas only that what you had loved
 thenceforth was inviolate quite,
And so I have only gone away. Seek not, for
 you never will find,—
Spend rather each precious moment in doing the
 work we outlined
For your brush if our Heavenly Father should
 call you back into the field,—
Strive on, and this present personal need, this
 ache in your heart, shall be healed,—
For me,—I shall think of you there in my home,
 I shall know that you dream of me still,
And shall read in each finished picture a starry
 sweet thought of

SAVILLE!"

SO HERE ENDETH THE STORY OF SAVILLE AS TOLD BY JULIA DITTO YOUNG AND DONE INTO A BOOK AT THE ROYCROFT SHOP WHICH IS IN EAST AURORA, NEW YORK, U. S. A. MDCCCXCVII

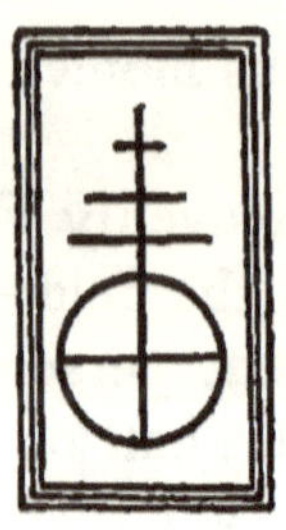

www.ingramcontent.com/pod-product-compliance
Lightning Source LLC
Chambersburg PA
CBHW020809020726
47495CB00008B/2651

* 9 7 8 3 7 4 4 7 0 7 8 9 3 *